What If

by Brittany Muttillo

Illustrated by Jayme Jacobs

Copyright
2021 Brittany Muttillo and Jayme Jacobs
ISBN 978-1-66786-869-1
All rights reserved, including the right to
reproduce this book or portions thereof
in any form whatsoever.

What If

by **Brittany Muttillo**
Illustrated by **Jayme Jacobs**

What If

This story was inspired by my niece, Rayne, our little wolf pup.
Remember forever, a wolf always stays with its pack.

To Jayme, my illustrator, but more importantly, my sister and
friend. Your brilliant artistry made this book come to life.
I cannot thank you enough.

Last, but definitely not least... To my parents,
husband, kids and friends; who always support me.
No limits, just unconditional love.

"A wolf always stays with its pack"
Rayne Wilson Jacobs, Age 7

"What if the other pups won't play with me mama? What if they run and I chase and I fall? What if they climb, but I can't cuz I'm small?"

"What if my eyes are too blue for the rest?
What if they laugh when I give it my best?
What if my fur isn't as soft or as gray?
What if I try, but I have a bad day?"

Mama looked up.
She saw the fear
and worry in the
eyes of her pup.

"Little love it's okay if they
don't play with you, you can't
control what they choose to
do."

She snuggled her babe and pulled her close,
she knew that this one was wiser than most.
"Your eyes, they sparkle like stars in the sky,
they are the bluest of blue so please don't
cry. Your soul is bright and shines like the
sun, now run along and have some fun."

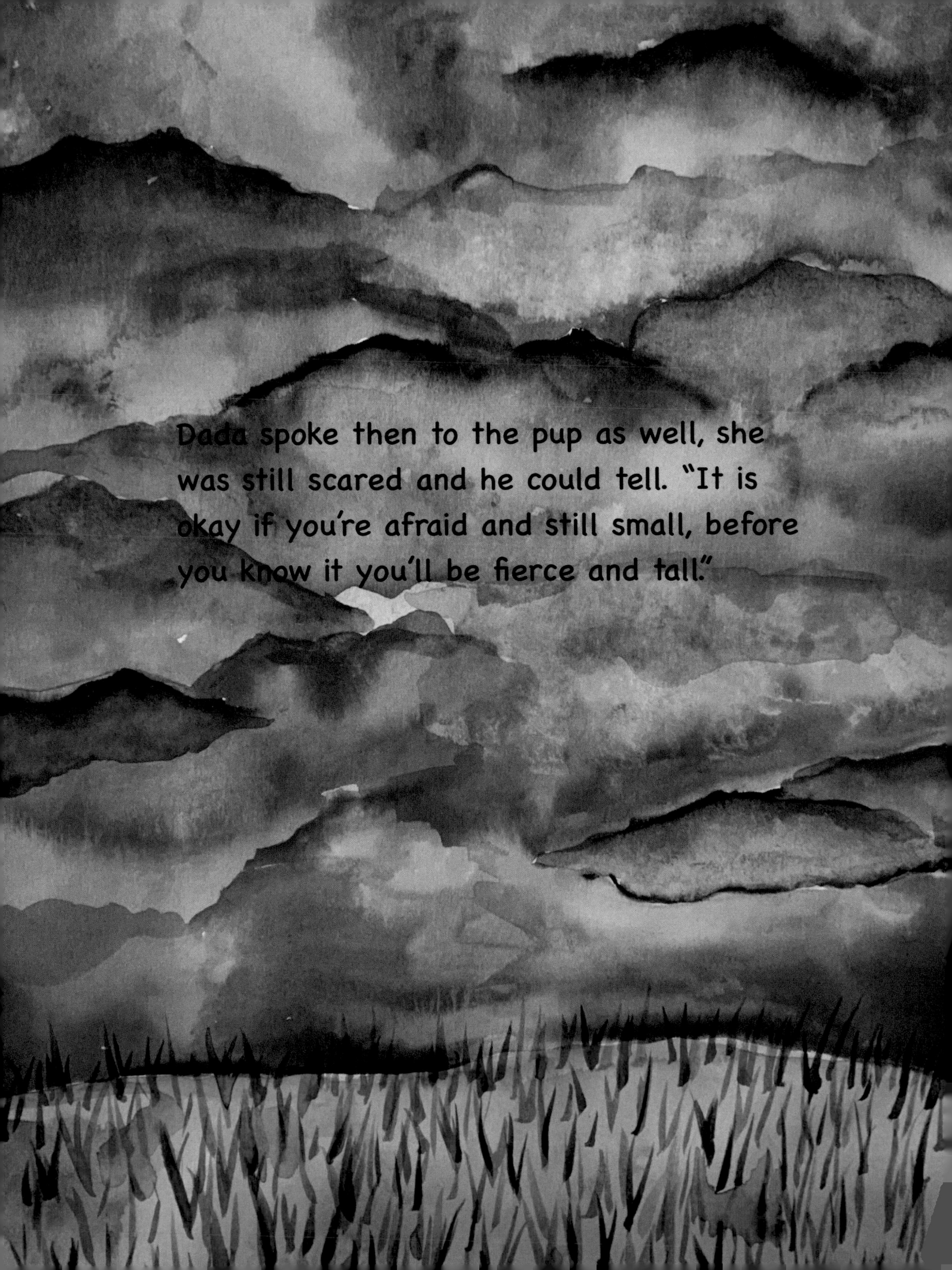

Dada spoke then to the pup as well, she was still scared and he could tell. "It is okay if you're afraid and still small, before you know it you'll be fierce and tall."

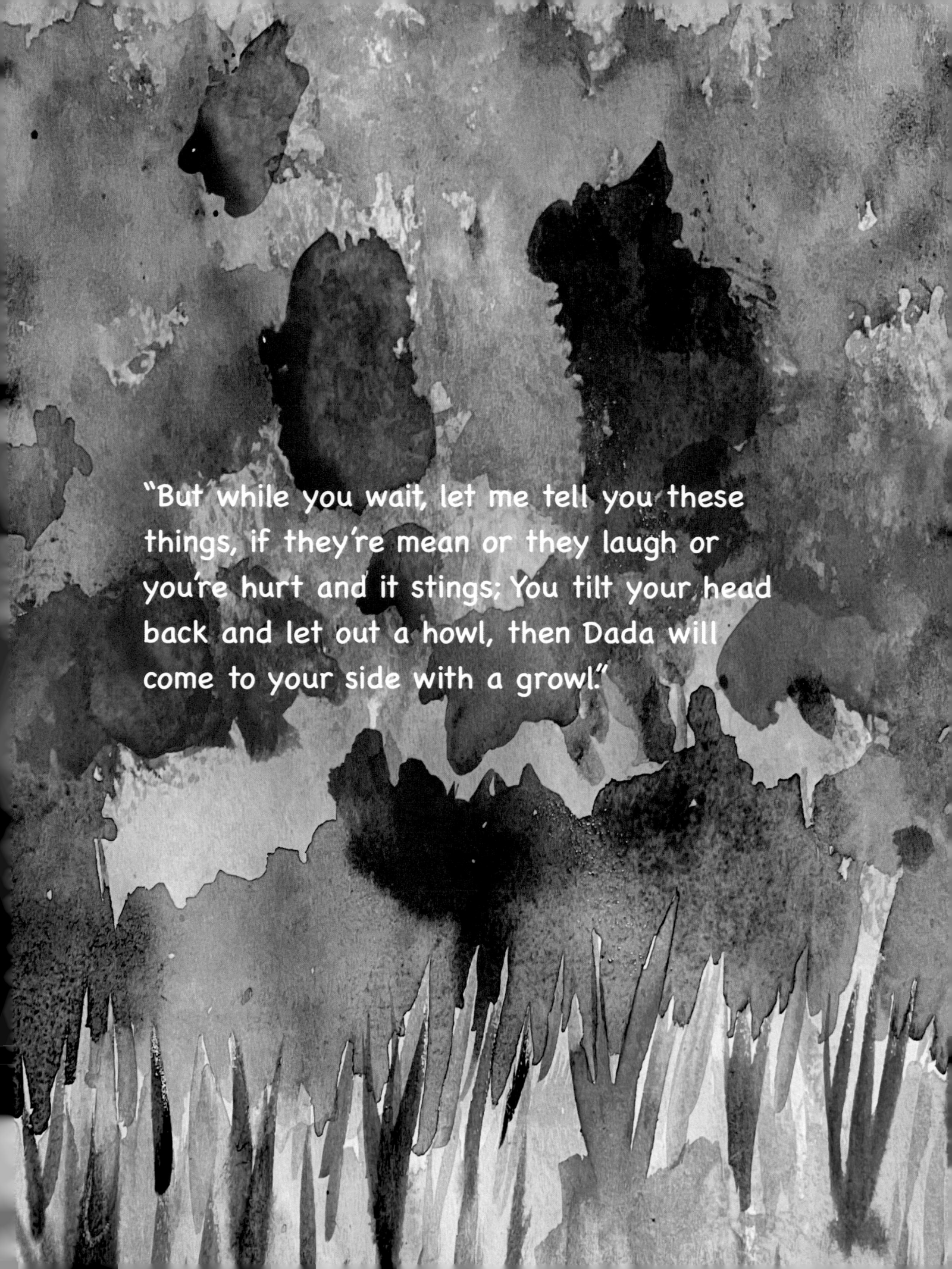

"But while you wait, let me tell you these things, if they're mean or they laugh or you're hurt and it stings; You tilt your head back and let out a howl, then Dada will come to your side with a growl."

"Your Brother and Sister, your Mama and me, we will be there whenever you need. Always remember we are your pack. Forget the rest, we have your back."

The End

Thinking Questions:

1. What emotion do you think the little pup was feeling?
2. Why do you think the little pup was feeling that way?
3. Is there anything you worry about?
4. Why do you think Mama wolf snuggled the pup?
5. What do you think Dada wolf meant by "pack"?
6. Who is in your pack?
7. Who do you go to when something is bothering you?
8. What do you think Dada wolf meant by "we have your back"?
9. What is one thing about your pack that makes you proud?
10. Do you remember the last time you had a great day?

About the Author

Brittany is first and foremost a mom. She was born and raised in rural Upstate New York, where she continues to reside today. Brittany finds a great amount of joy in spending time with her family and even the hustle and bustle that life with three kids brings. After earning her bachelor's degree in human development, Brittany joined corporate America and briefly put her dream of writing on hold.

Now that her children are older and her extended family continues to grow, she is more aware than ever that children need age-appropriate reading material they can connect with.

Brittany's stories bring to the forefront common childhood phenomenons and the key role families play in supporting children through those tough times. She hopes her books give families a way to connect that encourages emotional intelligence and creates a true bond, with positive reinforcement and understanding.

About the Illustrator

Jayme grew up in a small town in Central New York. She currently lives with her husband and three children just miles from her home town.

Jayme's gift of finding beauty in all things is unparalleled; she has the equally remarkable ability to capture that beauty on paper. With a background in art and adolescent education, she's able to use her water color paintings to bring magic into the hearts and minds of children. Jayme's hope is that through her illustrations, children see the world as the wondrous place it is and are inspired to create their own masterpiece.